# CONSERVING ENERGY

BY ELIZABETH THOMAS

Published by The Child's World®
1980 Lookout Drive • Mankato, MN 56003-1705
800-599-READ • www.childsworld.com

PHOTO CREDITS
Monkey Business Images/Shutterstock Images, cover, 1; Shutterstock
Images, 5, 15, 25; Michael Sleigh/iStockphoto, 7; Olivier Le Queinec/
Shutterstock Images, 9, 23; iStockphoto, 11, 17; Morgan Lane
Studios/iStockphoto, 13; Gary Whitton/Shutterstock Images, 19;
Elena Elisseeva/Shutterstock Images, 21; Anthony Berenyi/
Shutterstock Images, 27; Kai Chiang/iStockphoto, 29

CONTENT CONSULTANT
Jacques Finlay, Associate Professor, Department of Ecology,
Evolution and Behavior, University of Minnesota

ACKNOWLEDGMENTS
The Child's World®: Mary Berendes, Publishing Director
The Design Lab: Design
Red Line Editorial: Editorial direction

ISBN: 978-1-60973-172-4
LCCN: 2011927671

Printed in the United States of America in Mankato, MN
July, 2011
PA02090

# TABLE OF CONTENTS

Think of all the things you do that use energy: riding in a car, lighting a room, playing video games, or watching movies. Pretty much anything you buy takes energy to make. It takes energy to make a pack of gum, a plastic action figure, or a juice box. It takes energy to heat your home in winter and cool it in summer, to cook your food, and to dry your clothes.

We *need* energy all the time. So, why do we need to conserve it? The answer is two words: **fossil fuels**. Most of the energy we use every day comes from burning coal, oil, or natural gas. Burning fossil fuels causes pollution and too many **greenhouse gases** to go into the air. These gases trap heat inside Earth's atmosphere the way windows trap

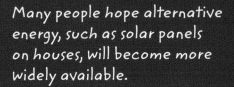

Many people hope alternative energy, such as solar panels on houses, will become more widely available.

heat inside a car on a sunny day. This causes **global warming**. Global warming could lead to rising coastal waters as polar ice melts.

Alternative forms of energy, such as wind or solar power, do not harm Earth. Until cleaner energy sources like these are more widely available, we need to learn how to use less fossil fuel energy. There are things you can do every day to help.

## **TIP #1**

# **TURN IT OFF**

When you are finished using a light, television, computer, or radio, flip the switch and turn it off! You'll help save energy every day with just a flick of a finger.

### **WHY?**

Where does your electricity come from? Chances are, it starts at a power plant that burns coal. Burning coal is one of the worst things for the environment. It gives off carbon dioxide gas, the leading cause of global warming. It also gives off sulfur dioxide, a toxin that contributes to acid rain. So, flipping that switch is one simple way to reduce the harmful effects of power plants.

Make it a habit to turn off the television when you're done watching it.

# KEEP THE DOORS CLOSED

Decide what you'd like to eat *before* you open the refrigerator door. After opening the door to the refrigerator, close it! That way you'll keep the cold in. If you open the door to the oven while cooking something, close it as soon as you can. Keep the heat in!

## WHY?

By keeping the doors closed, you keep the room-temperature air from warming up the refrigerator and cooling the oven. The refrigerator or oven won't have to use as much electricity to keep things cold or hot.

Remember not to keep the refrigerator or freezer door open while you prepare your food.

# KEEP IT COOL

In the winter months, ask your parents to keep the **thermostat** below 68 degrees Fahrenheit (20°C). If you get a little chilly, put on a sweater or curl up with a blanket. At night, the thermostat can be turned down even lower. You and your family will already be warm under the bed covers.

## WHY?

Your house is probably heated by burning some kind of fossil fuel, such as oil or natural gas. A thermostat set lower means less fossil fuel is burned. That means fewer greenhouse gases or other pollution go into the atmosphere.

Turning down the thermostat in your house saves energy in the winter months.

# READ IT ONLINE

If you find something on the computer that you enjoy reading, don't print it out. Read it right from the screen! Share it with your friends through e-mail. Or, even more fun, invite them over to read it with you!

## WHY?

Making paper gives off greenhouse gas into the air. It also causes air and water pollution. Recycled paper is an okay choice. Recycled paper uses half the energy of regular paper. It cuts back on greenhouse **emissions** by 40 percent. Still, compare that to using no paper. Reducing is always a better choice for the environment than recycling.

Reading online instead of printing out documents will reduce how much paper you print.

### THREE KIDS AND A SHRUB

When Adarsha Shivakumar and Apoorva Rangan visited their grandfather's farm in southern India, they learned the farmers nearby needed to grow a different crop than tobacco. The two learned that the oil-rich seeds of the Jatropha curcas shrub can be used as an alternative source of energy. The biofuel from these seeds can be used to run vehicles. It produces 80 percent less carbon dioxide than diesel fuel. The two siblings worked to help others plant 13,000 seedlings among 50 farm families in southern India.

# TAKE A WASTE-FREE LUNCH TO SCHOOL

Pack your lunch in reusable containers. Carry your drink or some soup in a thermos. Use metal silverware and then bring it home to wash. Bring a cloth napkin to wipe your mouth and hands. Bring it all in a reusable lunch bag.

## WHY?

In about the amount of time it will take you to read this sentence, more than 50,000 12-ounce (355 mL) aluminum cans were made. In the United States, people throw away about 2.5 million plastic bottles every hour! A lot of energy was used to make those items, and many of them eventually end up in a landfill. By bringing lunch in reusable lunch containers, you are helping to save the energy it takes to create those things.

> Pack your sandwich in a reusable plastic container instead of a plastic bag.

### SNAPPED OUT OF A SCHOOL TRAYS DAZE!

When a group of middle school students in Homer, Alaska, learned that the local landfill would be full by 2013, they decided to act. They proposed getting rid of the disposable trays in the cafeteria. The school is now using reusable plastic trays. The group has set up a recycling area in the lunchroom. After the first week, the school had reduced its amount of trash for the landfill by 50 percent. The group has prevented about 13,000 trays from being put in the local landfill.

# CLOSE CURTAINS AND DOORS

When it is cloudy and cold outside or when it is really hot, keep the curtains in your home closed. When you're entering and exiting your home, shut the door as quickly as you can.

## WHY?

Doing these things will keep your home warmer on cold days and cooler on hot days. The furnace, fans, or air conditioning won't have to work as hard to keep the air the right temperature in your home.

Keeping curtains closed helps keep your home cool on sunny days.

# SEE FOR YOURSELF!

Plan a visit for your class or school to take a tour of your local power plant. See for yourself how energy is created! Ask the tour guide if he or she knows any great tips to save energy.

## WHY?

Earth needs people to save as much energy as they can. But that's just one piece of the puzzle. Environmentalists also need to think big. They need to push for laws that encourage **conservation**. They need to push for energy options other than fossil fuels. You can become an environmentalist, too. The first step is to get educated. A visit to a power plant is a great way to get started.

Taking a tour of a power plant can help you learn more about using energy.

## TIP #8

# WALK OR RIDE!

Walk or ride your bike to places that are close by instead of having an adult drive you in the car. Cars burn fossil fuels. Your legs use renewable energy—yours!

## WHY?

Gasoline comes from oil, a fossil fuel. Gas-powered vehicles are a major producer of carbon dioxide. Even a 2-mile (3.2-km) car trip can add 2 pounds (.9 kg) of carbon dioxide into the atmosphere. By cutting back on using the car, you will be doing your part to stop global warming.

Riding your bike is fun, and it helps conserve the energy that would have been used in a vehicle.

**TIP #9**

# LOAD UP THOSE DISHES

If you have a dishwasher, don't wash dishes in the sink. Instead, fill up that dishwasher—the fuller the better—and start it. Make sure it's set to the energy-saving mode.

## WHY?

Some dishwashers use about 37 percent less water than washing dishes by hand. Saving water means saving energy. The biggest use of energy in most cities is supplying water and then cleaning it after it has been used. By saving water, you are also saving the energy it takes to pump it into your home and heat it up.

Only run the dishwasher when it is full.

# CHECK THE BULBS

Make sure all the light bulbs in your house are fluorescent bulbs. Most of these are the ones that look like spiraling tubes instead of rounded bulbs. Make sure your light bulbs are clean, too. Dusty ones use more energy.

## WHY?

An average household uses 11 percent of its energy budget on lighting. Fluorescent bulbs are four to six times more efficient than regular bulbs. They also last about ten times longer, so you won't have to buy as many of them. Fluorescent light bulbs give off 75 percent less heat, too. This could help in the summer. Your air conditioner won't have to make as much cool air.

CAUTION: HOT
RISK OF ELECTRIC SHOCK
WHERE DIRECTO EDIT[...]
NE PAS UTILISER AU[...]
LISTED 800V JE [...]

Fluorescent light bulbs
give off less heat and
last longer than regular
light bulbs.

# VAMPIRE ENERGY

Some electronics in your home suck up energy even when they're off. This is called vampire energy. One way to fix this is to use a power strip. When you're done using the television or computer, you can flip the switch to *OFF*. If you don't have power strips, you can unplug the devices, too.

## WHY?

Around 5 percent of energy used in the United States is wasted vampire energy. This is about the amount of electricity created by 37 power plants each year. That many power plants release more than 97 billion pounds (44 billion kg) of carbon dioxide into the air in a year.

Plug electronics and appliances into a power strip that stops vampire energy.

# PLAY OUTSIDE

Jump rope until you drop. Find out how far you can throw a Frisbee. Dig rocks out of your family's garden. Catch a firefly in your hands. Find out your favorite ways to play outside and play them often!

## WHY?

Think of the outdoors as a fun way to save energy. When you're playing inside, you're probably using electricity to light the room, to run a computer, and to play music or videos. Playing outside is completely electricity free!

Playing hopscotch instead of video games is a fun and easy way to conserve electricity.

# MORE WAYS TO GO GREEN

1. **Recycle** glass, paper, plastic, and cans. The more we recycle, the less energy will be used to dispose of these items or create more of them.

2. **Ask** your parents to help you plant a tree that will shade the house. The house will stay cooler and will need less air conditioning.

3. **Turn** off the faucet while you brush your teeth. It takes energy to clean used water.

4. **Use** both sides of a piece of paper before you throw it away.

5. **If** you do dishes by hand, turn the water off between rinsing each dish.

6. **Help** organize a carpool with your friends from school. Using only one car uses a lot less energy.

7. **Get** a group of friends together and clean up your local park.

8. **Instead** of using a leaf blower to pick up leaves, use a rake. Raking does not give off pollutants into the air.

9. **Wash** your clothes in cold water.

10. **String** a clothesline in the backyard and use the energy of the sun and wind to dry your clothes.

11. **Volunteer** to be an energy monitor for your classroom. You can make sure the lights and any machines are turned off when no one is in the room.

12. **Mow** the lawn with a push mower instead of cutting the grass with a gas-powered lawn mower.

**biofuel (BY-oh-fyoo-ul):** Biofuel is fuel that is made from raw biological materials. Biofuel causes less pollution than diesel fuel.

**conservation (kon-sur-VAY-shun):** Conservation is the preservation of the natural world. Energy conservation is important to keep Earth clean.

**emissions (i-MISH-uns):** Emissions are the release of things, such as chemicals into the atmosphere. Making recycled paper gives off less greenhouse gas emissions than making regular paper.

**fossil fuels (FOSS-ul FYOO-uls):** Fossil fuels are oil, natural gas, and coal, which formed from the remains of ancient plants. Reducing how much energy from fossil fuels we use is important.

**global warming (GLOHB-ul WOR-ming):** Global warming is the heating up of Earth's atmosphere and oceans due to air pollution. Too much carbon dioxide in the atmosphere increases global warming.

**greenhouse gases (GREEN-houss GASS-es):** Greenhouse gases are gases like carbon dioxide and methane that help hold heat in the atmosphere. Too many greenhouse gases in the atmosphere contribute to global warming.

**thermostat (THUR-muh-stat):** A thermostat is a device that senses the temperature in a room and turns on switches that control a furnace or air conditioner. Keep your thermostat turned down to conserve energy.

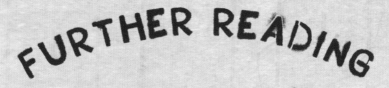

# FURTHER READING

## BOOKS

Bang, Molly. *My Light*. New York: Blue Sky Press, 2004.

Brown, Laurie Krasny, and Marc Brown. *Dinosaurs Go Green! How to Protect Our Planet*. New York: Little Brown, 2009.

Reilly, Kathleen M. *Energy Investigate: Why We Need Power & How We Get It*. White River Junction, VT: Nomad Press, 2009.

Rutty, Gregory. *Help Your Parents Save the Planet: 50 Simple Ways to Go Green Now!* New York: Play Bac Publishing, 2009.

## WEB SITES

Visit our Web site for links about conserving energy:
### http://www.childsworld.com/links

Note to Parents, Teachers, and Librarians: We routinely verify our Web links to make sure they are safe and active sites. So encourage your readers to check them out!